Tom Flies Hig.

by Jean Gilder

© THE MEDICI SOCIETY LTD · LONDON · 1991   *Printed in England.* ISBN 0 85503 164 6

One hot summer day Tom Badger and Billy Mole saw Mrs Rabbit hopping slowly along the path, carrying her small baby.

'Oh, Tom, I would like some nice fresh water,' said Mrs Rabbit, 'My baby is thirsty. There is only that nasty brown water to drink – at the bottom of the pond.'

'Yes,' agreed Tom, 'the stream is dried up too – I hope it rains soon.'

'It's not going to rain for a long time yet – we simply have to have some water soon!' exclaimed Billy. 'Tom, why don't you go and ask someone who KNOWS how to find water …' added the Mole.

Tom drew in a big breath.

'You mean Wanda the Water Diviner?' Tom was thinking hard. 'That's a good idea, Billy, but I don't know where she lives.'

'Let's ask Mr Chippy! said Mrs Rabbit 'I know he is working in the barn on High Point Hill.'

So they set off on the long climb to High Point Hill. When they reached the barn the animals could see Mr Chippy working inside. They peeped round the open door – what an amazing sight! Mr Chippy was struggling with an enormous mass of material and a huge basket.

'Ah! Just in time to give me a hand!' he called cheerfully.

'Help me take this outside – then we will fill the balloon with hot air from these …' He pointed to two large cylinders.

The animals all helped Mr Chippy to put the frame on the basket and join the balloon strings to the frame. Mr Chippy started up a fan, which gradually filled the huge balloon with air. Then he started the burners and the balloon billowed above them, tugging gently at the basket.

'Hop in quickly, Tom,' said Mr Chippy, 'and Mrs Rabbit and baby, and Billy – room for everybody!'

Mr Chippy lit the burners again and hot air roared into the balloon. Then he cast off the rope and they were off! Up they floated, higher and higher, and as they looked down they saw the trees and fields getting smaller and smaller.

'Whee – this is fun!' shouted Tom. Then he remembered why they had come to see Mr Chippy, and explained to him that they wanted to find Wanda, the Water Diviner.

'Well, I know she lives in a valley to the north,' said Mr Chippy '... so, as the wind is blowing us that way, we might ... Aha, what's that?'

There, to the north, was a mysterious-looking valley, green with trees, and a trail of smoke rising up straight through them. As they drifted over the trees, a lake came into view; in the middle of the lake was a tumble-down house built on stilts.

'That's it – that's where she lives!' called Mr Chippy, peering over the edge of the basket. 'Now, we'll try to land on that clear patch – hold tight, everybody!'

They descended rather quickly and landed – not with a bump, but with a big SPLASH! Ducks flew up all around and then they were floundering about in water-lilies.

To their surprise Wanda, the Water Diviner, and her pet frog Jumpy arrived in their punt to rescue them.

'Well, I've had a lot of visitors, but they usually come by boat!' laughed Wanda. 'Anyway, you had better come in and get dry.'

When they were all dry and warm after a drink of rose-hip tea, Tom explained why they had come to see her.

'We need some water badly,' he ended 'and we were told that you can find water in dry places.'

'Well, I would help you indeed, but I've lost the key to the cupboard where I keep my divining stick – I just don't know where it's gone,' she exclaimed with annoyance.

Suddenly Jumpy gave a funny little croak and tried to hide.

'Jumpy, do you know something about this?' enquired Wanda sternly.

'Yes, I hid the key because when you go out looking for water with your magic stick – you always leave me behind,' sobbed Jumpy.

'Oh, tell us where it is, Old Chap!' coaxed Tom. 'It's in a water-lily,' squeaked the frog, and he rushed out and dived into the lake.

There were thousands of water-lilies in the lake! Tom and the others tried to think what to do next. As Wanda sat with her chin in her hands, her head tipped forward.

'Your HAT!' exclaimed Tom, 'Please take it off – and look at the FLOWER!' He had seen the key – hidden in the lily that was on the brim of Wanda's hat!

Wanda opened the cupboard at last, and took out the forked hazel stick that she used to find water.

'I don't see how that can find water!' whispered Billy to Tom. 'You will see', murmured Wanda, who had overheard Billy, '… just come with me and you will see!'

They all climbed into Wanda's punt and slowly headed for the shore. 'Come on, Jumpy, you'd better come too,' called Wanda, and the little frog hopped joyfully into the boat.

It took a long time to walk to where the animals lived, and it was very hot and dry; Jumpy had a lift in Wanda's pocket-bag.

'Now then,' said Wanda 'everyone be very quiet please.' She held the forked stick out in front of her and paced slowly up and down. The animals followed her with interest at first, but gradually grew bored. 'I don't think that there is ANY water', whispered Mrs Rabbit.

Suddenly, the hazel stick jerked – up and down, up and down! 'Here – HERE you will find water!' exclaimed Wanda triumphantly.

The animals started to dig, but the ground was very hard and dry.

'Let ME try', said Billy Mole in his gruff voice. He worked hard with his special digging paws, and soon broke through the hard top crust. The others helped, and soon they were down quite a long way, but it was still dry.

'I don't think there's any water at all', said Mrs Rabbit sadly.

'My stick is NEVER wrong!' said Wanda firmly. 'Well, hardly ever', she added quietly.

'LISTEN' cried Jumpy, 'I *hear* water'. Sure enough, there was a tiny, tinkling, trickling sound. They all dug with renewed energy, and suddenly Billy Mole disappeared!

'Water!' he called, from the hole he'd fallen into, 'Lots of it!'

The animals peered over and saw water gushing out and forming a pool. They all bathed and drank with great delight. How delicious it was when they were so hot and thirsty!

Wanda was pleased to see she had been successful. 'Now you won't be short of water again', she said, 'but use it carefully and keep it clean!'

'Oh, we will, and thank you very much!' said the little friends all together.

That evening they had a barbecue party round their new pool, and much fun and laughter. Then Wanda decided it was time to return home by the light of the moon, and the animals accompanied her to the edge of the woods.

Mr Chippy went back with Wanda, as he wanted to rescue his balloon. When he had mended that, he stayed to help Wanda patch up her tumble-down house. Quite often when Tom and the animals were at the pool, they would wave to Mr Chippy and Wanda as they floated quietly by in the balloon – early in the morning, or sometimes in the evening.

THE END